Dear me

I hope this letter finds you in a moment of tranquility and self-reflection. I felt compelled to write to you today to express my sincerest apologies for all the hardships you have endured throughout your journey.

Firstly, I am sorry for the times when life seemed overwhelming and burdensome, when it felt as if the weight of the world was on your shoulders. I understand how exhausting it can be to face challenges head-on, to navigate through the uncertain and unfamiliar waters of life. I apologize for any moments when you felt unsupported or alone during those difficult times.

I am sorry for the moments of self-doubt that crept into your mind, whispering words of negativity
I apologize for the times when you made mistakes or experienced failures. It is an inevitable part of being human, and yet it can be incredibly disheartening. I want you to understand that these setbacks do not define you; they are stepping stones on the path to growth and self-improvement.

Chapter 1

My past experiences

You pushed me to my limits, challenged my beliefs, and tested my resilience. You brought forth moments of despair and uncertainty, causing me to question my strength and purpose. But through it all, I found the inner strength to persevere and rise above the adversities you presented.

You see, every obstacle you placed in my path became an opportunity for growth and self-discovery. Every setback became a chance to learn, adapt, and become better equipped for future challenges. Instead of allowing you to break me, I used you as stepping stones towards personal development and transformation.

You never broke me because I refused to let you define my worth or dictate my future. I refused to succumb to despair and chose instead to rise, stronger and more determined than ever before. Each experience, no matter how difficult, contributed to the person I am today.

Today, I stand tall and proud, knowing that I have emerged from the ashes of our relationship stronger, wiser, and more self-assured. I have learned to love myself unconditionally, to value my own worth, and to seek happiness from within. I have discovered that my strength does not depend on anyone else, but rather on my unwavering belief in myself.

Through the process of healing,
I learned valuable lessons about
love, trust, and self-worth. I
discovered the importance of
setting boundaries, both for
myself and in my relationships
with others. I realized that my
happiness should never depend
on someone else, but rather on
my own ability to love and
nurture myself. I became aware
that true strength lies in
embracing vulnerability and
embracing the journey of self-
acceptance.

So, no, you never broke me. In fact, you inadvertently played a role in shaping the person I am today. I am grateful for the experiences we shared, for they taught me the importance of resilience, self-love, and the power of letting go. I am no longer defined by the pain you caused me, but rather by the strength I gained from overcoming it.

So, Past Experiences, I
thank you for the
challenges, the tears,
and the moments of
doubt. I appreciate the
opportunities you
provided for growth and
the resilience you
instilled within me. You
may have tested my
limits, but you never
broke me.

Moving forward, I
carry the lessons
learned from you as a
reminder of my
strength and
resilience. I embrace
the uncertainties of
the future, knowing
that I have
persevered through
the trials of the past.
Together, we have
shaped and molded
the person I am
today.

Chapter 2

No longer shall we bear the weight of
pain,
Nor cling to shadows that cause our
hearts to wane.Normalize the act of
honoring our worth,
For in letting go, we unearth our own
rebirth.
So let us normalize releasing what's no
longer right,
To honor our spirits, to embrace the
light.
For in the act of letting go, we find
release,
And grant ourselves permission to find
inner peace.
Let go, dear heart, and let your spirit
soar,
For in detachment, new horizons shall
explore.
Normalize the wisdom of setting
yourself free,
To live a life where love and joy shall
always be.

when you find
yourself constantly
questioning where
you stand, the
intentions behind
their actions, or the
consistency of their
words, it may be time
to take a step back
and evaluate the
situation. Remember,
you have the power to
choose who you allow
into your life and
heart.

By letting go of those who leave your heart confused, you create space for the right people to enter. People who will communicate openly, treat you with respect, and bring a sense of peace and understanding to your life. It may be difficult at first, as emotions are involved, but trust that you are making room for something better.

Remember, your
happiness and emotional
well-being matter.
Surround yourself with
individuals who
appreciate and
understand your worth.
Embrace those who bring
clarity, support, and joy
into your life.
Have the courage to let
go of those who leave
your heart confused, and
trust that in doing so, you
are making room for the
relationships that align
with your true self.
Believe that you are
deserving of love,
understanding, and a
connection that brings
you peace.

Remember, you
have the power to
set boundaries,
prioritize self-care,
and surround
yourself with people
who uplift you.
Focus on cultivating
self-love and
treating yourself
with kindness.
When you embrace
your own worth, you
become less
dependent on
external validation.

Instead of waiting for others to treat you kindly, strive to foster a positive and compassionate mindset within yourself. It's liberating to let go of expectations and embrace the freedom of self-acceptance. You deserve to be surrounded by people who appreciate and respect you, but it starts with valuing yourself first. Take this opportunity to invest in your own well-being, pursue your passions, and build a fulfilling life that doesn't rely on the validation of others. Remember, you are worthy of kindness and love, and it begins within you.

Be kind to yourself,
with compassion
profound,
For healing requires
love, both gentle
and sound.
Nurture your soul
with self-care's
tender caress,
And let its healing
touch, your heart's
burdens address.

So, dear one,
remember this
gentle refrain,
When hope fills
your heart, or
healing causes
pain.
You are a vessel of
strength, destined
to rise,
With hope as your
compass, and
healing as your
prize

Let go, dear
heart, and let
your spirit soar,
For in
detachment,
new horizons
shall explore.
Normalize the
wisdom of
setting yourself
free,
To live a life
where love and
joy shall always
be.

Chapter 3

Today, I want to remind you of something incredibly important and powerful: You still have the ability to create a beautiful life for yourself, regardless of the years you may have lost to grief, darkness, or a wound that seemed to never heal. It's never too late to reclaim your happiness and embark on a journey of self-discovery and fulfillment.

Life has a way of throwing unexpected challenges our way, and sometimes these challenges can leave us feeling lost, broken, and hopeless. Perhaps you have experienced moments of deep grief, where the weight of your emotions seemed unbearable. Maybe you have battled with darkness, feeling trapped in a cycle of negativity and despair. Or perhaps you have carried a wound, physical or emotional, that has haunted you for far too long.

But here's the thing: You are so much stronger than you realize. The mere fact that you have endured these hardships and are still standing today is a testament to your resilience. It may feel like you have lost precious time, but every experience, no matter how painful, has the potential to shape you into a stronger and more compassionate person.

Grief, darkness, and wounds are part of the human experience. They do not define you. They are chapters in your life, but they are not the entirety of your story. You have the power to rise above them, to heal, and to create a life that is filled with joy, love, and fulfillment.

Take a moment to reflect
on the strength you have
already demonstrated.
Remember the times
when you found the
courage to face your pain
head-on, even when it
felt unbearable. Recall
the moments when you
reached out for support,
allowing yourself to be
vulnerable and open to
healing. Celebrate the
small victories along the
way, for they are the
stepping stones that will
lead you to a brighter
future.

It's important to acknowledge that healing takes time. It's a non-linear process, and there will be setbacks and moments of doubt. But don't let those moments define you. Instead, see them as opportunities for growth and self-reflection. Embrace them as lessons that will guide you towards a more beautiful and fulfilling life.

Remember, too, that
you are not alone in
this journey. Reach
out to those who love
and support you.
Seek professional
help if needed.
Surround yourself
with positive
influences and
engage in activities
that bring you joy
and peace. Cultivate
self-compassion and
practice self-care.
Give yourself
permission to heal
and to grow.

Remember, too, that you are not alone in this journey. Reach out to those who love and support you. Seek professional help if needed. Surround yourself with positive influences and engage in activities that bring you joy and peace. Cultivate self-compassion and practice self-care. Give yourself permission to heal and to grow.

The years you may
feel you have lost are
not lost forever.
They have shaped
you, taught you
valuable lessons,
and prepared you for
the life that lies
ahead. Even if it
feels like the wound
will never fully close,
trust that time and
self-care will
gradually bring
healing and
restoration.

Believe in your own
resilience and the power
within you to create a
beautiful life. Embrace the
present moment and the
endless possibilities it
holds. You have the
strength, the wisdom, and
the capacity for growth.
Trust in yourself, and step
forward into the future
with hope and
determination.

Chapter 4

One day, when you least expect it, life has a way of surprising us with unexpected encounters and remarkable connections. In a world that often feels chaotic and uncertain, it is comforting to believe that there will come a time when you will crash into someone who will be gentle with your heart.

Throughout our lives, we
encounter various individuals.
Some leave lasting impressions,
while others pass through like
fleeting shadows. But among
these encounters, there may come
a moment when someone enters
your life and changes everything.
This person will see through the
walls you've built, understand the
depth of your emotions, and
handle your heart with a
tenderness that takes your breath
away.

It's a beautiful notion, isn't it? To think that amidst the vastness of the world, there exists someone who will cherish your heart and treat it with the utmost care. This person will listen to your deepest fears and insecurities without judgment. They will hold your hand through life's challenges and celebrate your triumphs with genuine joy. They will offer a safe space for vulnerability, allowing you to share your hopes and dreams without reservation.

When this collision of souls occurs, it will be beyond your control. It may happen in the most unexpected of places—a crowded street, a local coffee shop, or even through the wonders of modern technology. The timing will be serendipitous, catching you off guard and leaving you breathless. It will be a collision of two hearts, merging together in perfect harmony.

This person will possess a
unique blend of kindness,
empathy, and understanding.
They will have a gentle spirit,
capable of soothing the
wounds that life has inflicted
upon your heart. Their
presence will bring about a
sense of calm and
reassurance, as if you've
finally found your anchor in
the stormy sea of life.

With this person by your side, you will experience a love that is patient and nurturing. They will appreciate your quirks and flaws, cherishing not only the best parts of you but also the parts that you often keep hidden. They will offer unwavering support and be your biggest cheerleader, encouraging you to pursue your dreams and embrace your true potential.

But it's important to
remember that this collision
of hearts cannot be forced or
hurried. It will happen when
the time is right, when both
you and this person are ready
to embark on a profound
journey of love and growth.
In the meantime, focus on
your own self-discovery and
personal development.
Cultivate self-love and
nurture your own heart, for it
is in this process that you will
become more open and
receptive to the love that
awaits you.

So, my dear friend, hold onto hope. Believe in the power of the universe to bring forth the right person at the right time. Trust that when you least expect it, you will crash into someone who will treat your heart with the gentleness and tenderness it deserves. Until then, continue to live your life authentically, embracing each day with an open heart and a spirit of adventure.

For in the collision of two souls, there lies the potential for a love that transcends time and space —a love that will bring you the happiness and fulfillment you've always yearned for. So keep your heart open, and have faith that when the time is right, love will find its way to you.

Chapter 5

Right now, maybe your
journey is about being
alone. It may seem
daunting and even
uncomfortable at times,
but it is a crucial phase of
self-discovery and
personal growth. Being
alone does not
necessarily mean feeling
lonely or isolated; rather,
it is an opportunity to
delve deep into your own
thoughts, emotions, and
aspirations. This journey
of solitude can be
transformative,
empowering, and
ultimately lead to a
greater understanding of
yourself and your place in
the world.

In today's fast-paced and interconnected world, solitude is often undervalued and overlooked. We are constantly bombarded with stimuli, distractions, and social pressures that make it difficult to carve out time for introspection. However, it is during these moments of solitude that we have the chance to truly connect with ourselves, our dreams, and our passions.

When you embark on a journey of being alone, you are giving yourself the space and freedom to explore your own thoughts and ideas without external influences. This solitude allows you to listen to your inner voice and discover your true desires, values, and beliefs. It is through this self-reflection that you can gain a clearer understanding of who you are as an individual and what you truly want from life.

Moreover, being alone provides an opportunity for self-care and self-nurturing. It is a time to recharge, rejuvenate, and focus on your own well-being. In the hustle and bustle of daily life, we often neglect our own needs and put the needs of others before our own. Being alone allows you to prioritize yourself and engage in activities that bring you joy and fulfillment. Whether it's reading a book, taking a long walk in nature, or practicing meditation, being alone gives you the chance to invest in self-care and cultivate a deeper sense of self-love.

Furthermore, being alone can foster independence and personal growth. When you rely solely on yourself, you become more self-reliant and resilient. You learn to trust your own judgment, make decisions based on your own values, and take responsibility for your own happiness. This independence is empowering and liberating, as it frees you from the expectations and opinions of others. It allows you to chart your own path and pursue your own dreams, regardless of societal norms or external pressures.

During this journey of being alone, it is natural to encounter challenges and moments of discomfort. Loneliness may creep in, and doubts may arise. However, it is important to embrace these moments as opportunities for growth. It is through facing these challenges head-on that you develop strength, resilience, and a deeper understanding of yourself. Remember, growth often occurs outside of our comfort zones, and being alone provides the perfect environment for personal development.

In conclusion, your journey of being alone is a valuable and transformative experience. It is a time for self-discovery, self-care, and personal growth. Embrace solitude as an opportunity to connect with your inner self, prioritize your well-being, and cultivate independence.

Embrace the discomfort and challenges that come with being alone, knowing that they are essential stepping stones on the path to self-fulfillment and a deeper understanding of yourself. Embrace the journey, for it is in solitude that you will find the strength, wisdom, and clarity to create a life that aligns with your truest self.

Maybe Right now, your journey is about being alone. It may seem daunting and even uncomfortable at times, but it is a crucial phase of self-discovery and personal growth. Being alone does not necessarily mean feeling lonely or isolated; rather, it is an opportunity to delve deep into your own thoughts, emotions, and aspirations. This journey of solitude can be transformative, empowering, and ultimately lead to a greater understanding of yourself and your place in the world.

In today's fast-paced and interconnected world, solitude is often undervalued and overlooked. We are constantly bombarded with stimuli, distractions, and social pressures that make it difficult to carve out time for introspection. However, it is during these moments of solitude that we have the chance to truly connect with ourselves, our dreams, and our passions.

When you embark on a journey of being alone, you are giving yourself the space and freedom to explore your own thoughts and ideas without external influences. This solitude allows you to listen to your inner voice and discover your true desires, values, and beliefs. It is through this self-reflection that you can gain a clearer understanding of who you are as an individual and what you truly want from life.

Moreover, being alone provides an opportunity for self-care and self-nurturing. It is a time to recharge, rejuvenate, and focus on your own well-being. In the hustle and bustle of daily life, we often neglect our own needs and put the needs of others before our own. Being alone allows you to prioritize yourself and engage in activities that bring you joy and fulfillment.

Whether it's reading a book, taking a long walk in nature, or practicing meditation, being alone gives you the chance to invest in self-care and cultivate a deeper sense of self-love.

Furthermore, being alone can foster independence and personal growth. When you rely solely on yourself, you become more self-reliant and resilient.

You learn to trust your own judgment, make decisions based on your own values, and take responsibility for your own happiness. This independence is empowering and liberating, as it frees you from the expectations and opinions of others. It allows you to chart your own path and pursue your own dreams, regardless of societal norms or external pressures.

During this journey of being alone, it is natural to encounter challenges and moments of discomfort. Loneliness may creep in, and doubts may arise. However, it is important to embrace these moments as opportunities for growth. It is through facing these challenges head-on that you develop strength, resilience, and a deeper understanding of yourself. Remember, growth often occurs outside of our comfort zones, and being alone provides the perfect environment for personal development.

In conclusion, your journey of being alone is a valuable and transformative experience. It is a time for self-discovery, self-care, and personal growth. Embrace solitude as an opportunity to connect with your inner self, prioritize your well-being, and cultivate independence. Embrace the discomfort and challenges that come with being alone, knowing that they are essential stepping stones on the path to self-fulfillment and a deeper understanding of yourself.

Made in the USA
Middletown, DE
26 December 2023

46808564R00031